UNEXPECTED STRANGERS
NOCTURNAL SCREAMS: VOLUME 5

Mark Leslie

STARK
PUBLISHING

Stark Publishing
March 2018 / Revised March 2021

Visit Mark Leslie on the web at www.markleslie.ca

To those who, despite the harshness in the world, make it possible for people to depend on the kindness of strangers

Table of Contents

Introduction

We have been warned, from the earliest days of our childhood, to beware of strangers.

That is what the lesson of several fairy tales, such as Red Riding Hood, tell us, after all.

In this fifth collection in the *Nocturnal Screams* series of short eerie tales, I thought it would be fun to collect together a few stories in which a fear of strangers, or an encounter with strangers, leads to darkness and nasty things.

From Out of the Night concerns itself with the fear of strangers approaching and threatening to intrude upon a home, and one woman's valiant attempt to face her fears head-on in order to protect her family from the terrors they are there to unleash.

The second story, *Captive Audience* imagines a seemingly innocent meeting of two strangers on a bus-stop bench; and what might happen if someone was so thirsty, so hungry for attention and companionship, that their very presence was almost vampiric in nature.

And, *Collateral Damage*, the third tale, concerns itself with a stranger in the audience of a club fantasizing about being friends with the comedian he is watching on stage. Except, the one lonely stranger carries with him a highly potent death curse for anyone he gets close to.

The tales you are about to read are perhaps along the lines of a *Twilight Zone* or *Outer Limits* or *Amazing Stories* episode if you will. If you're not of a certain age, you'll likely only know these old television shows via repeats and YouTube clips. You might liken the tales to something you may see on an episode of *Black Mirror* – only, my stories tend to involve less of the science-fiction element on that program and a lot more of the eerie and supernatural.

I go into a bit more detail, and I provide full *stories-behind-the-stories* for each of the tales, in a short section at the end of this book. That's where I'll reveal to you some insights behind the inspiration of the writing of each tale, as well as other insights that I think you might enjoy. That is, only if you're one who enjoys those behind-the-scene tales.

If you're not into that, then you're likely better off just skipping that part and enjoying the stories on their own.

And so, speaking of which, if you're a stranger to my fiction, then welcome, and thanks for checking this out. But even if you're familiar with my writing, perhaps you are still a stranger to the tales that I am about to share with you.

Please, take my hand and join me. I have some dark and eerie friends of mine that I'm just dying to introduce you to.

From Out of the Night

Although technology dominates *our world today, there still exist things that have been with us since we huddled in caves around brightly burning fires and avoided ominous shadows. Strange beings of the night become frighteningly real to us even now as we venture into the twenty-first century. Unknown things are still out there going bump in the night; a night where most of our dreams are nightmares. Scientifically, we have grown out of the dark ages, but our fears will forever remain among other frightened figures, jumping at shadows outside the cave.*

And perhaps for good reason . . .

*　*　*

Mary's screech from the kitchen came to Jack over a simple, old-fashioned baby monitor. "Here they come!"

Jack was in his basement den, putting the finishing touches on another promising non-fiction book about fear and the unknown. On the shelf before him sat several of his more popular published texts: One on Bigfoot, another on the Loch Ness Monster, several on U.F.O.'s, and then the books about a popular television series featuring a pair of FBI paranormal investigators back in the ninety's.

Upon hearing Mary's voice, he leaned away from the computer, ran his fingers along the base of the keyboard and then turned the screen off. Regretfully nodding to his unfinished project, he got to his feet and headed up the stairs.

Unseen by Mary as he reached the top of the stairs, he stood silently and observed his wife peering out the kitchen window. He studied her familiar features thinking of how often he saw her but didn't really look. Her worn face gave her the impression of someone much older than her forty-three years. She stood over the kitchen counter, silent for a moment. Her expression told him her mind was racing furiously.

When their teenaged son entered the room, Mary's head swung to orient on him, her face displaying a queer blank.

He gazed curiously at his mother.

"John, the lights!"

John clicked the kitchen light off in haste. He then moved to the front door and locked it." Are they back again, Mom?"

Mary gazed proudly at her son as he locked the door. "Smart move. And yes, they're back." She twisted to look out the window again. "There go a few of them now, to Mrs. Hancock's house. Oh, and there's another two coming up the other side of the street. Oh!" She ducked. "I don't think they saw me!"

"Why are there so many of them this time, Mom?"

"Because they're growing in strength and in number. They feed on our fear and prey on the weak-minded. They coerce others into becoming just like them. And they won't be satisfied until everyone is a blood-thirsty, flesh-eating demon like they are. They won't stop until everyone has *Become*."

A burst of laughter filled the room and Mary jumped, swinging her head in the direction of the living room. A smile of relief crossed her face and Jack could tell, even before she spoke, that it had only been the canned laughter of a television sitcom audience.

"Susie!" Mary shrieked. "Turn off that TV!"

The television continued to play. Another wave of laughter from the studio audience flooded the darkened room.

Mary turned to face her son, a barely controlled panic in her eyes. "Listen, John. Take your sister and go down to the basement. Tell your father to shut off his den lights and you hide with him there. I don't want those cannibals to get anywhere near you two. Do you hear me?"

As Jack watched them, a wave of nostalgia overcame him. It was so obvious her only concern was for her children. She was willing to sacrifice herself for them without a second thought. It made Jack pine for the days when their own love had been so unselfish. But that had been years ago, before their relationship had evolved into something more mature, something increasingly less demonstrative. It was nothing like his active love for his writing. It was simply there.

While John went into the living room to get his little sister, Jack moved silently into the kitchen. His eyes met Mary's as the light and noise of the television stopped. In a thickened darkness they looked at each other and listened to their children stumble to the stairway.

"I love you," Mary whispered at their sounds in the dark. When they were gone she addressed her husband. "The kids'll be safer down there, hidden away. *They* won't have access to them."

"Why don't you go downstairs with the kids, hon?" Jack suggested. "Let me handle them tonight."

"No. I'm not defenceless. I can protect my family just fine. Now get yourself back downstairs and look after my children. They're going to need someone with them."

"Mary, please," he said, reaching out to touch her shoulder. "I can protect us."

Flinching back from his touch, Mary glared at him. "No. No, you can't. If you'd wanted to protect us, you would have put the boards up like I suggested."

"We don't need the boards, Mary." Jack thought back to the year before when she'd insisted that he nail boards on all the windows and doors. They'd stayed in the boarded-up house for three days. Fortunately, the kids were able to get an online hook up to their classrooms, so they didn't miss school. And Jack's writing work hardly had him leaving the basement den, never mind the house. So, it hadn't been that much of a hardship. But he couldn't justify using the boards this year. The nuisance was just too much this time. His manuscript was already overdue, and his agent was calling three times a day; twice less than his editor.

"Yes, we do need the boards. The boards were probably the only thing that saved us last time." She crossed her arms and paced the length of the kitchen, careful to stay out of touching distance. "What about Mr. and Mrs. Allen two doors down? They didn't board up their house last year and look what's happened to them. They're changing, they're *Becoming*. They may not be consuming flesh yet, but you can tell they've started to change. You can see it in their eyes. *Becoming* doesn't happen overnight, Jack. It has to grow and fester inside them over time. It's a horrible process of self-induced pain and suffering."

"Mary, I honestly don't think it was because of the boards. We'll be perfectly safe without them."

"You're right, the Allens were weak. Ted and Lisa just couldn't resist their supernatural charms and promises of immortality. But they wouldn't have had to resist them had they boarded themselves up inside." She peeked out the window once more. "Oh damn! We forgot to turn off the outside porch light. Quick, get the switch. Get the switch!"

Jack reached for the light switch.

"Too late!" she cried. "Too damn late! A group of them have already spotted the light. They're drawn to it like moths, Jack. Like sick, disgusting insects." She swallowed noisily and ran a hand down the side of her face. "Looks like I'm going to have to finally face them. Well, at least you and the kids will be safely hidden."

Jack stepped forward, feeling guilty. He couldn't even remember the words of comfort he used to be able to find for her when she'd needed his strength. Despite the urgency of the situation, the desperation in her voice, his mind kept wandering back to his unfinished manuscript. No matter how hard he tried, he honestly wanted nothing more than to go downstairs and continue writing.

Feeling like a poseur, he tried again. "Mary please. Go downstairs and let me handle it."

"No. You don't know all their tricks, Jack. They have to be invited in. They can only corrupt those who invite them in. There's no need for all of us to be exposed to their horrors. Besides, I'm the strongest minded. Maybe they won't be able to convert me into one of them. I should be strong enough to resist them."

"You're right," Jack sighed. She was right, too. She was one stubborn lady, impossible to sway once her mind was set. He knew that all too well. "I know you can do it. I'll go downstairs and wait with the kids. Good luck, Mary." He headed for the basement stairs.

"Wait, Jack. Before you go, promise me something."

He paused on the top step.

"It would kill me to corrupt my own family, but that's what they do, that's how they survive, isn't it? By making others like them? Promise me that if, after this meeting with them tonight, if I *Become*, you'll take the children far away from me. Promise me you'll do everything you can to prevent the kids from *Becoming*. Promise me that."

Jack took a deep breath. "I promise."

A heavy knock sounded through the darkness. "This is it." She leaned back against the counter and sighed. "I'll wait a minute and make sure you're safely hidden. I love you."

A tear came to Jack's eye. He brushed it away. "I love you too, Mary." The words rolled off his tongue like a forgotten language. He quickly moved down the stairs.

When Jack got to the den, he closed the door behind him and sat in the armchair near the computer. Susie ran over to him, jumped into his lap, and threw her arms around him. She was trembling.

Over the baby monitor, he could hear Mary's footsteps upstairs as she moved to open the door. Turning the monitor off, he frowned as he attempted to suppress a chuckle. "It's all right, Susie. It's okay. Mommy's going to be okay."

She looked at him questioningly and found courage in her father's eyes and voice. Jack was slightly irritated at how Mary's behavior had frightened their daughter. John understood what was wrong with his mother, but Susie, being four, was still too young to make sense of it.

All she knew was that mommy was scared to death of those *Christians.*

The Christians, with their non-scientific belief in life after death, resurrection of the dead, and their weekly consumption of another man's flesh and blood.

Mary was a perfect wife and mother in all other respects; so, what was so wrong in having one paranoid delusion? It was natural. In fact, Jack based his living on other people's paranoid delusions and fears. Paranoia and fear helped to feed his family. And besides, it was a simple harmless paranoia.

It's not like Mary would ever hurt anybody.

Suddenly inspired, Jack put his daughter down and told the children to watch the television in the room across the hall so long as they kept the door closed and the volume low.

He brought his hands down gently on the keyboard, and, smiling, he wrote what he felt would be a satisfying conclusion to the introductory chapter.

* * *

Irritation occurs in the true believer's heart when science or the reason of daylight find rational ways of knocking their beliefs and fears. But given the fact that proving the non-existence of anything is virtually impossible, fears continue to haunt us. We are pursued from out of the night by dreams of the unknown and visions of the unexplainable – the unreal.

Even if, one day, proof is given that our fear-created beings do not actually exist, we will probably invent new ones.

* * *

The doorway to the den opened, startling Jack out of his reverent typing. He looked up as Mary's throaty laugh filled the room.

"I did it, Jack," she said. "I protected my family from them. They're never going to get us now."

Mary stood in the doorway clutching a blood-stained butcher knife and smiled a bright white-toothed grin at him from beneath the coat of deep crimson on her face.

He looked at her a moment and realised the frightening truth.

There were no more monsters out there.

Ghosts, vampires, witches and bogeymen had all been vanquished. Monsters, creatures of the night and ghouls had all been conquered, and there was no need to create new ones. The only monsters left were the ones inside our own hearts. The demon thoughts that allowed Mary to obsess over something she was afraid of until the insanity finally consumed her; the spirits of selfishness that allowed Jack to simply overlook her problems because he was too busy focussing on himself and his writing.

These personal monsters that people never want to face, were the only nightmares left.

These thoughts, his most brilliant conclusion yet, would never make it to the printed page, because for the first time in eight years, Jack completely forgot about his writing as he got up, went over to his wife and held her while she wept.

Captive Audience

Sean regarded his watch and shook his head as the unmerciful sun beat down on the unshaded bus stop bench. As was usual for this time of year, the bus had probably overheated somewhere down the highway. Last weekend when he'd taken the bus into the city to pick up a week's worth of writing supplies, he'd ended up waiting four hours before the old rusty hunk of metal finally arrived. It had had to stop three times to cool down the engine.

Blinking the sweat from his eyes, Sean watched a chubby middle-aged man saunter toward the bus stop. Sean didn't know the man personally but knew that his name was Rupert.

Everybody knew Rupert.

He was the town bore.

Sean had never spoken with him before, being new to the little town of Overbrook, but Rupert's reputation preceded him.

Apparently, Rupert would corner people at the library or grocery store and manipulate them into conversations that they wanted nothing to do with. According to Sean's next-door neighbor, getting out of a conversation with Rupert was a difficult, learned process, on par with getting out of the heat in the middle of this tiny desert town.

Sean sighed as Rupert neared the bench. As a writer, Sean needed all the different kinds of input from the world he could get. Perhaps a discussion with Rupert would provide fuel for a character in a novel some day.

As it was, Sean couldn't duck out now, anyway.

Despite the heat of that August afternoon and his long-sleeved sweater and thick corduroy pants, Rupert wasn't sweating. He smiled at Sean as he sat down on the faded and paint cracked bus stop bench, slid his sweater sleeves up his arms and thrust his pudgy fingers into a bag of potato chips.

The rustling of the bag immediately caught Sean's attention.

He'd just eaten a late breakfast before leaving the house, but the hunger returned as if signaled by the junk food being eaten before him.

Still looking at the chips, Sean wiped sweat from his forehead. Hopefully the bus wouldn't be so late this week. His newly acquired hunger had him longing for lunch. There was a fast food establishment with the best submarine sandwiches in the city right beside the business supply store in the mall. One of those subs would certainly hit the spot.

Rupert looked at Sean for a moment, staring at him in the same manner that Sean stared at the bag of chips. Then he sprang forward on the bench as if suddenly kicked.

"Oh, do you want some?" he said, offering the chips.

"Sure, thanks," Sean said, accepting the handful Rupert poured him.

Rupert brought one stubby hand up to the chin of his round, pumpkin-shaped head. Sean heard a distinct and loud saliva smacking sound in Rupert's mouth just before he spoke again.

"You know, speaking of those Nazi extremists there, Sean, I was reading in *Time* magazine about the institution of a Klu Klux Klan in Vancouver. It's sort of like the institutionalization of propaganda that could be traced to small patches across the United States near the end of the last World War." He paused to brush his thick blond hair from his face. "So far, there have been five malicious threats on the so-called minority groups in that metropolitan area."

"What do you mean by malicious threats?" Sean asked, struggling to keep the corners of his mouth even. Without even a cursory greeting, Rupert had launched into some far-fetched topic as if the two of them were already discussing the subject at length. Sean wondered if Rupert had been having the conversation in his head and, to him, the words exchanged with Sean were simply a natural extension. Whatever the case, Sean felt the foreboding sense of becoming trapped in one of Rupert's infamous one-sided, large-worded conversations.

Another saliva-smacking sound announced that Rupert would be speaking again. "Well, the, ah, defacement of public property and spray painted anti-Semitic slogans, you know, that kind of happening."

Out of ritualized courtesy, Sean nodded, pretending to be interested.

Hopefully, the bus would be full when it arrived, and he could escape Rupert on the chance that there would not be two adjacent seats available. Until then, though, he had to stick it out as best he could.

"Has anyone been injured in these . . . happenings?" Sean asked, crunching down the last of his handful of chips.

"Well, I didn't have the time to really get into the article, there, Sean, but from my first initial glance I would assume that some lives have been blatantly badgered, to say the least." Leaning over sideways on the bench, Rupert did the saliva-smacking bit once again. "You know, people like that just make me want to resign from the human race."

"Yeah," Sean replied, eyeing the chips once more. "I know what you mean." Sean thrust his hand out for some more chips, and when Rupert didn't take the cue, he poked the man's chubby leg.

"Oh," Rupert said, looking at Sean's upturned palm. "Want some more chips?"

Sean nodded, and Rupert dumped the rest of the bag into his hand. The chips simulated Rupert's payment for making Sean listen to his boring chatter.

No, not boring, because the subject matter was interesting and socially significant.

It was the way in which Rupert discussed it. Almost as if all he wanted to do was present his views in a sophisticated manner. No, not just sophisticated. How would Rupert put it? *Bullshitified*.

Having paid off his conversational prostitute, Rupert immediately jumped back into his monologue. Sean, in turn, shoved the whole pile of chips directly into his mouth.

"Anyway, like I was saying there, Sean: Today there's just too much hatred in our society. It's like we're facing this downward post-millennial spiral into some Dantanien hell."

His mouth still stuffed, Sean felt a laugh welling up inside.

There Rupert went again, using large words that Sean was certain he had to have made up. In an effort to control his laugh, the mouthful of potato chips slipped down his throat.

He sucked in, trying to swallow them, but the rising impulse of laughter held the sharp pieces of the potato chips lodged in place, cutting off his oxygen.

He brought his hands up to his neck, squirming on the bench.

"I have a theory about this 'Inferno-come-reality' that we're facing as society continues to deal with massive changes and bi-partisan hatred that's tearing society apart." Rupert said, excitedly rolling his sleeves past his elbows. "I mean, sure it has been almost two decades, but the millennium is still young, and it takes time to adjust. It all comes down to a basic conceptualization of self — and with that the understanding of the essential human need.

"Do you know what I mean?"

Sean's arms flailed wildly, his face a dull blue color.

Why didn't this guy notice he was choking?

Rupert continued. "Once we understand our own needs and existential desires, there, Sean, we'll have a better understanding of others. We'll learn to observe and care for their feelings just like they were our own.

"Once that becomes established, the rest of the so-called puzzle of humanity will fall right into place. It's really a simple matter when you give yourself enough time to think about it."

Pausing, Rupert gazed over at Sean. His arms no longer flailing, Sean's face was pale, and his eyes were bugged out wide, staring at Rupert.

His bladder and bowels having released upon his death, Sean stunk.

The afternoon heat didn't help.

Rupert didn't concern himself with that. Sean's wide bugged out eyes were signs to Rupert that he was listening in quiet awe to Rupert's theory.

No one had ever done that before.

Rupert smiled and flipped his hair back from his forehead. No one had ever listened to Rupert for more than a few minutes. Finally, he had a captive audience in Sean.

A small stirring, not unlike an electrical charge, raced through Rupert's body. It was like an awakening of sorts. For a moment, Rupert recognized the power flowing through him, washing over his being — then it was gone.

He paused, pursing his lips, considering the next thing he would discuss. When the idea came to him, he made the lip smacking sound.

Rupert went on and told Sean about his theory of alternate universes, about how he felt the Nielsen Rating system really worked, about disguised triple reverse sexism in modern Western society, and every other theory he'd ever constructed in all of the lonely and quiet hours he'd spent by himself his entire life.

He finished his theorizing and had enough time to stuff Sean's body into the bushes behind the bus stop bench before the bus finally arrived.

As the bus slowly pulled up, Rupert stood from his spot on the bench, took a look at the vacant bus and then turned his head back to smile at the bus driver.

The bus driver, Ben, was hot and sweaty from yet another eventful morning. This forty-minute trip into the city was going to be the death of him, he was sure, since the bus had overheated at least twice and the air conditioning was no longer working.

Oh well, he thought, at least I'll have some company on the trip from here on in.

He lifted his sweat dampened sleeve to wipe more beads of the salty thick fluid from his forehead, and eyed the bottle of water in Rupert's right hand.

He blinked hard when he spotted it, as he could have sworn just moments ago that the man sitting on the bus stop bench hadn't been holding anything at all.

Rupert climbed onto the bus and held the water out to Ben.

"Thirsty?" he asked.

Collateral Damage

1

I'm not a scavenger," Peter mumbled as he rifled through the jacket pockets of the dead man who lay crumpled against the alley wall. "I'm a sin-eater."

He had to keep telling himself this.

After all, scavengers feed on the dead. Peter fed on the living, was the force that took those lives. With each victim he could feel their life-force draining from them and channelling through his entire being, kick-starting orgasmic ripples of uncontrollable laughter that shot up and out from some dark core.

Peter was the harbinger of death.

He had been for years; and though he had suspected he was to blame for so very many deaths – his mother, during childbirth, his father just a few years later, his very first best friend, Donnie, then a dozen more friends, colleagues and teachers at school – it had just been in the past six months that it had become undeniable.

His stare killed people – it sucked the life-force right out of them.

He had spent several frustrated years trying to deny it and wailing in the pain of being at the centre of so much loss and tragic death; loved ones whose lives were cut short simply for their proximity to Peter O'Mallick.

He had tried to put an end to it.

Several times.

But for some reason, perhaps a side-effect of the curse that coursed through his veins, every single suicide attempt had proven fruitless; simply, he could not die by his own hand.

It was only recently that Peter realized this power, this inexplicable curse he had been born with, could be put to good use.

In an alley, one not unlike the one he was in now, he had accidentally killed a man; watched the side of his head explode when making eye contact with him. But, while standing over the dead body, again frustrated with his curse, he had discovered the man he had just killed had himself been a killer.

That changed everything.

It meant, finally, after all those years of *suffering the slings and arrows of his outrageous fortune*, Peter could *attempt to take arms against his sea of troubles*, apply his curse to a good cause, and prove to Hamlet that it didn't have to always be end in tragedy.

If he was cursed with causing death, the very least he could do was focus his time and energy on ridding the world of the low-lives, the carrion who fed off of the havoc, pain and loss of others.

That moment, the Peter O'Mallick who had railed against his curse took a back-seat to the new Peter who had embraced the power flowing within him as a force of good.

He had become a vigilante.

Stalking the dark alleys of Toronto, he had been able to pick away a living, living on the streets, avoiding crowds, homeless shelters or interacting much with others. He had seemed to have a natural instinct for finding the low-lives who fed off of society, sought to harm, hurt, steal and kill. And those were the people he unleashed his power on.

People like the dead man whose jacket pockets Peter was digging through. This man was part of a gang who had been threatening local shopkeepers with a "protection racket" by extorting cash from several businesses on Gerrard Street near Church.

It was funny how most people – not even low-lives like this extortionist – didn't pay any attention to the homeless when going about their business. Peter had been lying low, spending time in this particular neighbourhood as part of his regular roaming, never staying in one area for too long, particularly not after making a kill, when he had picked up on the man's activities.

He had watched this man, a stocky man with a red beard, and his partner, a lean, tall bald man who wore over-sized CHIPS-style reflection sunglasses, make their way through the neighbourhood shops, spending just a few minutes going inside each one.

Peter had lived long enough on the streets to understand they were up to something more than wanting to visit each shop – particularly when they returned each day.

After spotting them making their way through the exact same routine for the third day in a row, Peter planted himself inside the small pita shop, using pocket change to buy a bottle of water and then sit at one of the round tables and wait for one of them to make his way inside.

The shop owner greeted the red-bearded thug with a nervous smile, made him a shawarma unasked which was handed over without the exchange of money and said: "I pay, I pay. You keep me safe. Thank you," nodding nervously the whole time.

The extortionist glanced over at Peter, who was dressed in filthy, ragged clothes, and immediately dismissed him as a derelict and no threat to his business.

"That's right, Paco," the thug had said. "You pay, and you stay safe for another day."

At that point, Paco wiped his hands on his apron, popped the cash drawer open and handed the man a couple of green bills.

"Good boy, Paco," the bearded man said, sinking his teeth into his shawarma. Then, with a mouthful, mumbled, "See you again tomorrow."

Peter followed Red-beard out the pita shop, up Mutual Street and down an alley behind an auto service store. He waited for the man to come back out after doing his business there when he confronted him.

"Excuse me," Peter said to him when red-beard came back out of the rear staff entrance to the auto service bay, licking sauce and meat juices from his fingers. "May I have a word with you?"

"Fuck off," red-beard said with a dismissive wave, barely even looking at him. "Go and bum change off of someone else."

"That's not what I want," Peter said, taking a few steps closer.

The man kept walking toward Peter, shaking his head and reaching down to move his jacket aside, revealing the gun handle sticking out of the left side of his pants.

"I said 'Fuck off!'" the man said, now just a couple of feet in front of Peter and looking right at him. "Fuck off and die, or I'll pop a round in between your filthy eyes."

"I'll fuck off," Peter said, standing his ground as the man finally made solid eye contact with him. "But you're the one who's going to die."

Peter stared back at the man and felt the power of the death stare channeling through him and right into the man's being.

Red-beard's eyes widened in a sudden realization of terror and the hand poised over the handle of the gun suddenly clenched into a fist, as if the man was being seized by some sort of electric shock.

His left hand clutched at his chest as he fell to his knees, then dropped to the ground, his face making a loud smack as it connected with the pavement.

The uncontrollable reflexive laughter that came with each death bubbled up through Peter's throat and he released it like some satisfying post-death consumption burp.

A full-on shiver ran through Peter's body as the laughter ended, and he sunk down on one knee over red-beard's dead body.

As Peter crouched and rolled the man over, digging through his pockets, he reminded himself that he wasn't a scavenger.

He was a vigilante.

He was ridding the streets of the scum of society, cleansing the world of those who sought to hurt, to maim, to kill.

And in order to survive, he needed money. So he took it from the bad guys he put out of commission.

The way a carrion eater picked the flesh off the rotting bones of a dead animal carcass.

He shook his head, waving the thought away, and repeated the mantra to himself.

"I'm not a scavenger, I'm a sin-eater."

He still only partially believed it.

2

Michael paced back and forth in the tight space backstage, feeling the familiar rush of adrenaline with knowing that, in just a few minutes, he would be out there and at the mercy of the crowd.

His palms were slick, and his heart was racing; just enough to get him in the proper groove for a stand-up routine. He hadn't been to Toronto in years and wanted to ensure he knocked off a few jokes specific to Canada and to this city.

Local crowds always liked when you could do that.

He bounced a few times on the balls of his feet, feeling his heart rate get to the perfect state he needed it to be in before going on stage. It was all part of the routine, part of the set-up.

Michael had always loved comedy, particularly improv, and though he worked a full-time job he had pursued his passion with almost every free moment.

Jokes, one-liners and amusing observations came to him constantly, typically while he went about his every-day tasks. He had long been making note of them to use in his stand-up routine, had even sold some of his jokes to both Carson and Leno back in the day.

But he lived for the thrill and fun of being on stage, working the crowd, holding them in the palm of his hand. Continuing to pace, he waited for the host to introduce him, glancing at his watch one more time. The previous comic had gone over-time by a few minutes, and the host, who had already been operating in a deficit, went well over the five-minute segue. That put the whole evening close to 10 minutes behind.

Michael had to take a deep breath and not let that get the better of him.

He reminded himself to focus on the crowd on the other side of those curtains, the jokes he would be telling, the wonderful moment of anticipation.

Finally, he heard the host finish off his bit and begin to introduce him.

"Ladies and gentlemen, all the way from Buffalo, New York, the one, the only, Michael C. Bass!"

The crowd applauded politely as the host went down the steps on the side of the stage and Michael stepped out from the break in the curtains.

"Good evening!" Michael said, trying to make out faces in the crowd under the harsh glare of the lights. It always took about a minute or so for his eyes to adjust, and he liked to pick a few people from the front row to gauge how he was doing.

He opened with a line that typically worked on winning over a Toronto audience.

"It's great to be back in Toronto: Tee-0h, The Big Smoke, Hogtown, Little York, Hollywood North – or, as I like to call it, home of the CN Tower, North America's tallest erection."

The crowd tittered satisfactorily, so he moved on.

"Seriously, you've got to love a city that constantly inflicts penis envy on all of its neighbors."

More laughter.

"I've only gone up in the CN Tower once. That was enough for me. I'm not a big fan of heights. I never have been. I think it stems back to my first trip to Disney when I went on the Space Mountain ride. My daughter, who knew of my aversion to heights, warned me about it, but I didn't listen to her. I'm not sure if you're familiar with the Space Mountain roller coaster at Disney, but it's mostly in the dark; so I figured, if I couldn't see the height, it'd be okay.

"When the EMS team had to revive me at the end of the ride . . ." he paused to let the laughing subside, ". . . my daughter was standing there shaking her head. I also heard her mutter to the stranger beside her. 'Gee, Daddy, what's wrong with that man?'"

He paused, again, to let the audience digest that one, waited for the laughter to settle down, then continued.

"I've always been afraid of heights. Seriously, the 70's were terrifying for me, with all those platform and elevator shoes. Aw, heck, who am I kidding? There wasn't much about the 70's that I liked.

"Okay, there was one thing I liked about the 70's. The Paul Newman movie *Slapshot*. Are there any hockey fans in the crowd tonight?"

The crowd hooted and hollered.

"I love hockey. I think that's why I love Canada so much. Canada is serious about its hockey. Am I right?"

The crowd shouted their agreement.

"I've been a serious hockey fan my entire life. For me, it's a big deal. I go all out, wear a full suit and tie to each and every game I go to. And if I can't make it to a game, I'll sit there in my living room dressed to the nines. For effect, I even have a few friends over to cram beside me on the couch, thrust giant foam fingers in front of the TV to block my view, and spill beer and popcorn all over me.

"Being from Buffalo, I'm a Sabres fan," he paused for the expected boos and a few odd cheers. "But when I'm not cheering for my home team, I'm rooting for the Toronto Maple Leafs." *More cheering from the crowd, as expected.*

"I love the Toronto team. About the only thing that bothers me about these guys is the name. The proper plural term is "Leaves" not "Leafs" – but that's okay, they can get away with it, because of how many Stanley Cups the team has won in the past 40 years. No, wait, nix that. Well, at least the team has a snazzy blue and white uniform.

"What is it with fan loyalty to a team that hasn't won the cup since 1967? That's die-hard fandom and you've got to love that commitment. I think it's one of the reasons I love Maple Leaf fans: there's a sense of pride in working your ass off, putting your shoulder to the wheel and keeping at it, despite the odds."

The crowd cheered loudly at the compliment, and Michael basked in the rhythm he had fallen into.

There was something satisfying about manipulating a crowd, a deeply personal sense of accomplishment to bring mirth to complete strangers.

Unbeknownst to Michael, one particular member of his audience was laughing out of joy at his jokes rather than as the uncontrollable reflex to taking someone's life.

3

The sound coming out of Peter's throat had felt foreign and odd, but also strangely comforting.

It was pure, simple, mirth-inspired laughter.

When was the last time he had done that?

This Bass character was good. And a wonderful diversion from the mission that had brought Peter into the comedy club this evening.

Peter had followed the lean tall bald man here, having lost him for several hours after dealing with red-beard. It wasn't until the early evening that Peter had spotted him again.

Before Peter had been able to get the man alone, Baldy had slipped in to this comedy club.

Rather than wait outside, Peter figured he would head in, try to get a bite to eat and make the best of his wait.

Tucked away in the furthest corner of the crowded club, determined to avoid making eye contact with anybody, Peter focused on his mark while wolfing down a greasy burger and fries.

Baldy sat right up front, laughing loudly at every quip.

It wasn't until this Bass guy got on stage that Peter felt himself beginning to actually enjoy the comedy on stage.

There was something about him that Peter liked.

He imagined this Bass fellow would be a fun-loving friend.

It was an interesting fantasy, but the thought reminded Peter of just how long it had been since he had had a friend.

All of his own friends were either dead or far enough away from Peter to now be safe; at least to the best of his knowledge.

Because the deaths that Peter caused hadn't all been instantaneous; some of them had taken longer to manifest.

Like the cancer eating away at Sarah's father.

Sarah.

Peter felt a sharp stab of pain when thinking about her, about the tender moments they had together, about the long-ago dreams they'd shared about their common future, about the talks late into the night while they held each other and swore they would always be there for one another, about making love to Sarah while looking her deep in the eyes.

That was the clincher.

Sarah was missing and presumed dead. She was last seen here in Toronto, mixed up in some sort of drug-related activity; at least that's what it looked like, based on the fact that she was last seen with her cousin, whose body was found abandoned in a downtown alley, dead from a drug overdose.

That was originally what Peter had been doing here. Living on the streets, looking for any sign of Sarah, but also working his way through the darker part of society and attempting to use his death curse to make a positive difference.

He had to, after all, make up for all of those innocent people his curse had taken over the years.

So many deaths. So many loved ones; so many friends.

Peter rejected the thought of becoming friends with this Michael C. Bass.

It simply wouldn't be a good thing. Not if this Bass fellow wanted to stay alive.

Nobody who Peter cared about seemed to survive becoming close to him.

Which further highlighted Peter's dilemma. He needed to find Sarah, to know that she was alive, to ensure she was okay. But he couldn't get close to her again for fear that the growing curse ripening inside him would kill her.

The thought that Sarah was still out there, still alive, was the one thing that kept Peter going, kept him focused, and able to deal with the memories of so many deaths.

Peter's train of thought was broken when he spotted Baldy getting up.

Was he leaving the club?

Baldy headed off to the restrooms, so Peter relaxed again for a moment, deciding to pick at the fries on his plate and finish them off. If Baldy left, after all, Peter would follow him. And it was best to eat this rare meal while he could.

He focused his mind back on the stage.

The comedian was riffing on a new topic now.

"I'm honest to a fault," Bass said. "And it doesn't really win me many friends.

"When a woman asks if a dress makes her look fat, I give her the God's honest truth. 'Like a hippo,' I say. Of course, I'm simply honest, but not mean. If I were mean I'd go on to say. 'It's not really the dress, honey. It's your gigantic ass. That's what the real problem is here. The dress is fine. It's your huge ass that makes the dress look fat.'

"But I don't go that far. I'm honest, not cruel.

"My friends have often wondered what the C in my name stands for. I tell them 'Collateral' – as in 'Collateral Damage.'

"I can't keep my honesty in check, particularly when there's a joke to be had. So sometimes, in pursuit of a laugh, that next funny one-liner, there are unintended victims. Collateral.

"But humor is good. Laughter brings goodness to the world. And honesty is good, too. So making humor out of honesty, bringing a little more good to the world, makes that little bit of collateral damage acceptable."

4

Peter was following the comedian's latest chain of dialogue so closely that he almost didn't notice Baldy's exit. But he did manage to spot him out of the corner of his eye and tracked his movement. Baldy had moved from the hallway that led to the bathroom and ducked along the corridor that appeared to lead backstage.

Peter considered his unfinished fries, aware of how rare it was that he had a square meal. But he couldn't stay to finish them – he had to keep on the bald man's trail.

He got up, made his way across the bar and headed toward the corridor Baldy had taken. When he got to the end, there was a left turn that led to the back-stage area and a right turn which led to a series of doors, likely the office, a couple of dressing rooms and perhaps a green room. All of the doors were closed.

Peter decided to turn left.

He took only a few steps, could still hear the comedian, Bass, performing his routine on the other side of the curtains, but he also heard something else.

A hollow dragging noise.

He stopped to listen.

Something was being dragged across the floor. And it was coming from the dark shadows on Peter's right, just around the corner from where he stood.

He waited a moment, hoping his eyes would adjust to the light, then stepped forward and peeked around the corner.

Baldy was turned away from Peter and dragging a large topless cardboard box back away from the corner. The three-foot-high box, a couple of feet across and wide, was filled to capacity with what looked like stage props, signs, lighting fixture supplies and other occasionally used stage and backstage objects.

When Baldy finished dragging this box out, he moved around it to push a larger wooden crate along the wall.

What the hell was he up to?

Peter's curiosity got the better of him, and, instead of making his move, he kept watching.

Baldy finished shoving the crate aside, he knelt down in front of a vent in the wall, pulled something out of his back pocket, what appeared to be a jackknife, and used either the blade or a flathead screwdriver attachment to pry the metal vent grate out from the wall.

Then he reached inside and pulled something out.

It appeared to be a handgun.

Shit.

Peter realized he only had a moment to surprise Baldy without the risk of being shot, and was about to step fully around the corner when a loud and familiar voice from behind startled him.

"Hey, Bub, what's going on?"

Peter turned and saw Michael Bass, the comedian, standing a few feet behind him, a bemused look on his face. He must have finished his on-stage act and was heading back toward the greenroom.

"Shit!" Peter said, about to warn the comedian to get the hell out of there.

Still on from the stage, or perhaps because he was always "on" Michael replied. "Shit? If that's what you're looking for, you've taken a wrong turn, my friend. The men's room is just back thataways."

"No," Baldy said stepping up between them, the gun trained on them. "You've both taken a wrong turn."

"What the hell?" Michael said, automatically thrusting his hands up in the air.

Baldy positioned himself a few feet away, the gun in his left hand slowly sweeping back and forth between Peter and Michael.

Peter stared at Baldy, squinting hard, trying to get the man to look into his eyes. But it didn't seem to be working. Either it was too dark, and the man couldn't see his eyes, or Baldy was distracted, his eyes flitting quickly between Peter and Michael. Perhaps it was a combination of both, but Peter's curse, his power, didn't seem to be working. He figured he needed to get Baldy into a lighted area.

"Hand over your wallets and you won't get hurt," Baldy said.

"You don't want to do that," Michael said. "All I have is US money, and with the exchange rates the way they are you're not really going to get a good value. Might I suggest-"

But Baldy cut him off by reaching out and smacking him on the side of the head. "Knock it off! I said hand over your fucking wallet."

Peter used that distraction to move.

Not being a person of action – his idea of sports was playing interactive video games on the Wii or Xbox 360 Kinect – Peter had never really been in a fight before. But having been a child of the television era, having watched hundreds of action movies, in particular, the entire Karate Kid series as well as virtually every single superhero flick ever made, he seemed to know somewhat what he could do to quickly disarm Baldy.

Or so he thought.

He took a few steps forward, successfully knocking Baldy's gun hand to the side with an outward swing of his right arm and charging into the man's chest with his left shoulder.

Baldy stumbled back, into a tall wooden backdrop, a bit off balance, but still on his feet.

The gun was still in his hand.

So much for my career as a superhero, taking out bad guys with a single attack, Peter thought.

Baldy regained his balance and trained the gun back on Peter.

"Enough bullshit," he said.

The sound of a couple of people talking echoed from the hallway that led to the greenrooms and the office.

"Shit!" Baldy said.

"As I mentioned, the men's room is-"

"Shut your pie-hole!" Baldy said, cuffing Michael in the head, then turning and running to the far side of the stage and running out a door with a bright exit sign.

"You okay?" Peter asked Michael, who nodded that he was. "Good. Stay here, get help. I'm going after him."

Peter then ran for the exit, pushed his way through the door which wasn't yet half-closed, and saw that it led to an exit, likely to the alley, and a set of stairs going up. His thought was that Baldy would have headed outside, but the door was closed, and, he noticed, had an emergency exit alarm bar on it.

So, Baldy hadn't gone out; he must have gone up.

Peter paused, listened and could hear the sound of footsteps echoing from up the stairwell.

Baldy was moving fast.

Peter hoofed it up, grabbing onto the handrail to pull himself around each corner.

The sound of Baldy's footsteps continued to echo through the stairwell, meaning he hadn't stopped at any of the levels on the way up. Despite being out of breath, Peter did his best to keep running.

Baldy was faster than Peter, and by the time Peter had ascended what seemed at least a dozen floors, he had to pause and catch his breath. The sound of Baldy running hadn't abated, so Peter pushed himself to keep moving forward, despite the knife of pain in his side and his own loud panting sound echoing through the stairwell.

A few minutes later the sound of running footsteps coming from above stopped, followed mere seconds later by a loud thud and CRACK.

He tried to put on a bit more speed.

When he finally reached the top of the stairwell, and stood, breathless, beside the door at the top, he noticed the broken padlocked latch, figuring it was likely an entrance to the roof.

Peter estimated they were about twenty stories up.

He slowly pushed the door all the way open.

Baldy wasn't anywhere within sight on the part of the roof Peter could see from the doorway.

He stepped out from the doorway, looking to his left and right, and, not seeing anything, wondered if Baldy had jumped to an adjacent rooftop.

The answer came quickly and without warning, in the form of a heavy body slamming into his lower back from above and behind. Peter stumbled forward a few steps then crumpled to the rooftop as the weight of a full-sized man pushed down on his upper back and shoulders.

As he fell, the blow of the gun handle striking him on the back of the head felt like it had meant to be a direct hit, but was likely reduced in intensity by the angle of the two falling men.

Lucky he had crumpled so quickly, Peter thought.

Then he was on his knees, Baldy still on top of him.

Peter rolled forward, hoping to toss Baldy overtop of himself.

It only partially worked. Baldy was still half on Peter's back, sending another punch. This time the man's naked right fist struck at the back of Peter's head; and this time it connected, sending a bright flash of pain through Peter's vision.

He let out a yell, buckled, and managed to knock Baldy most of the way off of his back. He kicked out, his foot connecting with Baldy's left shoulder. Baldy's gun clattered a few feet away on the rooftop.

Peter knew he only had a few seconds to get up, get the upper hand on Baldy. It might have been dark in the backstage area, but at least there was ambient light from the taller nearby building windows casting down onto the rooftop. Light enough for Baldy to be able to see Peter's eyes, to feel the wraith of his death curse.

Peter took a few steps back, closer to the edge of the building, closer to a part of the roof that would cast more light on him.

Baldy got up, and took a few steps backwards, pausing to reach for the gun. Then he turned and pointed it at Peter.

Their eyes met.

And that's when Michael appeared in the doorway, just a few feet away.

"I thought it over," Michael said, his hands already thrust into the air, as he stepped out of the doorway. "My US cash might not be worth that much, but you look like a smart fellow. I figure you'll put it away, hang onto it, watch the markets and exchange it for Canadian funds once the economy shifts back to normal."

Baldy turned, facing Michael, aiming the gun at him. Michael winked at Peter and smiled, their eyes meeting straight on for the first time, Peter getting a clear view of Michael's eyes, Michael having a clear view of Peter's.

No! Peter thought. But it was too late when the thought came into his mind.

"Fuck off with those stupid jokes," Baldy said, and pulled the trigger.

A loud explosion of gunfire shattered the night air and a small pimple of blood sprouted on Michael's chest. He looked down at it, a look of complete shock on his face.

"You . . . shot . . . me . . ." Michael said as if arousing from a deep sleep; then, his quick wit suddenly surfaced and he said. "And ruined a damn fine shirt, I might add."

At that, Michael stumbled forward, directly toward Baldy, his arms out, as if stepping forward to embrace the thug in a giant bear hug.

Baldy stood there watching Michael lumber forward and collapse right into his arms. The two shuffled backwards on the roof as if they were an ill-matched novice student and dance instructor awkwardly practicing a routine neither knew to the wrong music.

Then then took two more steps backward, right to the edge of the roof, and they both dropped off.

Peter ran to the edge, in time to see the two bodies slam in unison into the top of a garbage dumpster in the alley below.

Despite his breathlessness, the uncontrollable laughter bubbled up from the base of his stomach and filled the night air with an insane stream of cackling.

It lasted almost half a minute, and when the mad burst of laughter finally subsided, Peter took a few steps forward and peeked over the edge. He looked down at the street twenty-odd floors below at the two dead men, their bodies still intertwined like star-crossed lovers, and shook his head.

Sure, he took the bad guy down, but why did his curse also have to kill an innocent man?

It was a senseless waste of a good life.

But at least Baldy was taken out.

What was it that Bass had said when he'd been on stage?

Something about collateral damage. *That bringing a little more good to the world, makes that little bit of collateral damage acceptable.*

The world now had one less good guy, but also two less bad-guys.

Acceptable collateral for a day's work.

"I'm a sin-eater," Peter mumbled, walking away from the edge of the rooftop. "A harbinger of death."

Behind the Screams

Many of the emails and comments that I receive from readers share that they quite enjoy the "behind the story" notes I regularly add to the end of many of my short stories and collections of short fiction.

And so, I present here, a few insights and some background information either on the inspiration or source for each of the stories you have just read.

If you're not a person who enjoys watching the special features on a DVD or the movie along with commentary from the actors or director, then I suggest you simply stop reading now. Thanks for picking up this collection and reading a few of my stories. I hope you enjoyed them enough to want to read more of my fiction.

If, however, you do enjoy that "behind the curtains" peek into my fiction, then we still have a little bit of time left in our little post-midnight stroll. Just ignore those dancing shadows trailing along beside us, and let me bring your attention to some further background and insights into the tales you just read.

About "From Out of the Night"

Originally published in The Darker Woods #2, 1997.

This particular story came to me when I was in my teens. And the first draft of this story was written some time when I was likely sixteen or seventeen.

I was in the living room and my mother was running around the house shutting the curtains and closing the front door. She was slightly panicked and, considering that I had a hyper-active imagination, I was wondering what could possibly be outside during that near-dusk time period that she was so afraid of. What evil stalked our house from outside that we had to hide and protect ourselves from?

"What is it?" I remember calling to my mom in a panic.

"It's the Jehovah Witnesses," she said. "I don't want to have to talk to them."

Even though the threat was an uncomfortable conversation with some charismatic and genuinely nice people trying to force their religion on others, the idea that there was something truly evil stalking the house from out of the night stayed with me.

That inspired me to start writing a tale where I was imagining that there might be some sort of vampiric creatures turning people into them, if only they could be invited into their homes.

A chill ran down my spine. Always a good sign that I'm on to something. If it gives me a chill, perhaps it'll give a reader a chill, too.

But even as I was writing the story, I kept reflecting back on my Mom's reaction and how it had startled and concerned me.

What if there was a woman who was genuinely frightened, perhaps even terrified, of anything remotely religious?

How might that affect her family?

Would they humor her? Would they tolerate her occasional lapse of reason?

The very first draft of this story was a simple tale, but as I was writing it, I realized that Mary was delusional, and so I had the husband, John, be the additional point of view to help the reader slowly realize that. In the first draft, John was downstairs watching television in the family room and she sent the kids to be with him. It was a simple tale of Mary being crazy and the relief and "twist ending" was that there were no monsters, she had just imagined them.

So, when I finished that first draft, I went back and wrote the introductory italicized text piece. It was my ode to the Rod Serling moment, when, on episodes of *The Twilight Zone*, he would walk out and provide some introductory text to the story you were about to read, and then maybe have a few concluding words. Or maybe it was like the Crypt Keeper in those old "Tales from the Tomb" style horror comics I enjoyed reading so much when I was a kid. But in either case, I liked that element of the story. It reminded me of the many books about monsters, ghosts and other eerie phenomenon that I enjoyed reading about.

In the original version of the story, the tale ends with the italicized bit about the fact that as science disproves our belief of some monsters, we'll simply invent new ones. That was, after all, the point I was trying to make.

And in my second and third drafts of the story, I wondered a little more about John. Why would he let his wife believe the things she did? Well, because it was his livelihood; that's why! John made his living selling books about monsters and ghosts and UFOs and goblins and demons and other paranormal creatures. It works in his favor if more people believe; so, he sits back and believes it's for the best to let her, and others, have delusions, because it helps him sell books.

I wanted to paint him as a little more cold and calculating in that updated version. Show John as looking at his wife as an experiment that he can write about in his non-fiction books about paranormal topics.

The introductory and then concluding paragraphs were meant to be reflections of writing from the book John was working on.

And so, the original completed version of the story ended with Mary facing the religious people and John having a bit of a laugh at her expense.

But when I submitted the tale to the small press magazine *The Darker Woods*, editor Stephanie Connolly wrote back to me and said she likely the tale, but she wanted to see a little more character development, particularly within the relationship between Mary and her husband John. She also wondered if I might introduce a real danger. What if Mary's obsession was dangerous to herself and to others? Because she thought this was a life-and-death situation, what would happen if Mary reacted accordingly?

The sign of a great editor is when they ask the writer just the right questions to pull even more out about their characters and the situation.

Those were the exact right questions.

I went back and added more to the relationship; made John realize the coldness of his ways.

And then I wrote the final scene, with Mary showing up with the bloody knife.

And that's the breaking point – far too late, of course – when John realizes the tragedy that he let happen because he was thinking only of himself and of his writing.

A much more shocking, bloody, and yet emotional ending.

Thanks to the advice of a brilliant editor.

Thank you, Stephanie!

An additional aside to this story that I find absolutely amusing, is that, though I wrote the initial story when I was a teenager and the re-write when I was in my mid-twenties and had only had a few short horror stories published at that time, I went on to become a little bit like John, in my story.

In 2014 I wrote my first non-fiction exploration into the paranormal: *Haunted Hamilton: The Ghosts of Dundurn Castle and other Steeltown Shivers*. I was living in Hamilton, Ontario, at the time and had been inspired to write it based on the local historic ghost walks of the city. And this became the first book of true ghost stories (or "true" ghost stories, depending on your perspective) I have penned. As of the writing of this, I have five more non-fiction paranormal books out (titles that include *Creepy*

Capital, Haunted Hospitals, Spooky Sudbury and *Tomes of Terror)*, and a few more in the works.

Though I still write and enjoy fiction, I've found a minor calling in documenting "tales told as true" about ghosts and other eerie and unexplainable events.

I did not marry a woman who was psychotic and terrified of religious people.

But at least one element of the character of John indicates an intriguing case of fictional people I wrote about becoming at least part of my own reality.

About "Captive Audience"

A slightly different version of this story previously published in Champagne Shivers #3, 2007.

The very first version of this story, much like "From Out of the Night" was written when I was in high school.

I grew up in a small town in mid-Northern Ontario. Our high school had about 300 people in it. And so, when I was in Grade 13, (yes, I was from the last set of Grade Thirteen students from Ontario – the fifth year of high school), I wanted to take a Grade 13 level Creative Writing English class. Our school only offered a single standard English class, which I took; but I wanted the creative writing one as well. I met with the guidance counselor to discuss this request (because I knew that there were courses that existed that would fulfill my desire) and he hooked me up with a correspondence Grade 13 level creative writing course with a teacher from Toronto.

This was, of course, pre-internet, so I rec'd my workbooks and assignments and mailed my work back and forth between myself and my teacher. She was an amazing teacher. I learned so much from that course and from her.

One of the assignments I had to work on for the course was a character sketch assignment.

The idea was to show, through dialogue, and through action, two different characters interacting.

I drew, as inspiration, something I had witnessed in the Grade 13 lounge at my high school.

Sean, a jock and one of the cool kids of the school, was sitting beside another fellow who was a bit of a nerd. The nerdy fellow was trying to engage Sean in a stimulating and intellectual conversation (far beyond the realm of the conversations most seventeen-year-olds might have at the time); but Sean was only feigning interest in his conversation so that he could dig into the bag of Hickory Sticks the nerd was eating and sharing. (Hickory Sticks, for my non-Canadian readers, are a style of potato chip that are thin, much thinner than the small McDonald's French fries, that were hickory-smoked and very popular. The vending machines at our high school always had them in supply).

So the story, initially entitled "Ponderous," was merely the disinterested jock talking with the nerd. But they weren't really talking. The jock was pretending to listen and wasn't really involved in the conversation, and the nerd never realized that the jock was just using him; he was just happy to be running on about some subject he was fascinated with, no matter if any else was listening or not.

I came back to that story a few years later, likely during university when I was supposed to be studying or reading or something other than toying in the fictional worlds I enjoyed escaping into.

And I saw something I could do to re-work that short and somewhat darkly funny scene.

What if Rupert had some as of yet undiscovered paranormal ability to have accidental things happen to somehow impair the person he was speaking with and, in effect, bore them to death?

Boring a person to death was a fun and unique dark concept.

So, I re-crafted both his character as well as Sean's and imagined how an accident might help Rupert come to subtly realize the power that he has always held within him.

And that Sean would be the first of a multitude of victims he might bore to death.

It is interesting, reading this story today for inclusion in this collection, how much of what I had Rupert talking about applies to today; it was based on actual over-heard conversation from the late 1980s.

The story was written as a horror tale in the mid-1990s and then, re-drafted and submitted to a market in the mid-2000s where I, again, updated the story to the first century of the new millennium.

Of course, for this reprint of the tale, I slightly tweaked it into the second decade of the new millennium, and also tweaked a few more words to reference the horrific and nasty split between the left and the right, particular in America; but it's certainly something that is having an effect in Canada, the UK and other nations of the world – we are, after all, truly a global community in so many ways.

I don't think I'm done with the concept of a person being able to bore someone to death. So I'll likely write about it again. (Heck, if you're NOT interested in this particular back-story, perhaps I'm having that effect on you, now. Insert smiley face here).

I like Rupert. Despite the evil side-effect of what he ends up doing to people, I feel for him, for his loneliness and his desire to just have a meaningful conversation with someone.

I never truly drew this out in the story, but it was always my belief that if someone just truly actually listened to Rupert, if they engaged with him, they'd be fine. The supernatural power of "boring a person to death" only happens when they don't engage.

I think I was trying to say something about the danger to society when that happens.

Which is why I don't think I'm done with this concept, even though Rupert, and this tale, is a simple self-contained story.

About "Collateral Damage"

Originally published as a limited edition (100 copy) chapbook and eBook in 2013.

I love to kill people.

I know this is something that horror and mystery and thriller authors get to say; because we do it on a regular basis in our fiction.

But in the writing of the character of Peter O'Mallick, I have killed real people several times. And I've even raised money for a good cause while doing it.

Peter O'Mallick is the character of a horror novel entitled *I, Death*.

He was born, like the other stories in this collection, from writing I originally did when I was in high school. Peter was created in a "freewriting" exercise that I did in Grade 10 during an English class at Levack District High School. The teacher, Gary Furhman, reserved about a half an hour once per week in English class for a time slot where students had to write something – ANYTHING – on a sheet of paper and hand it in at the end of the half hour. It could be a story, a poem, an essay, a journal. Heck, it could be a doodle or just their signature.

Whatever they wanted to write. They just had to write something.

I usually took advantage of those times to write a short story. Typically, a short-short story.

And one of the tales I wrote was a story in the form of a simple fake journal of a suicidal teenager named Peter O'Mallick who believed that he was suffering from a death curse. The tale was about 1000 words.

Several years later, when I was in University, I wondered what might have become of Peter, so I wrote a story set a few years after that I called "Sin-Eater." It was interesting to see what had become of him.

But even then, I couldn't get Peter out of my head.

A few years after that I was looking at how I might combine the stories "I, Death" and "Sin-Eater" into something a little bigger.

That's when I decided to blog, from the POV of the angst-filled teenager and share Peter's story. I knew how the story would start; I also knew a few elements about what would happen on his journey; and I knew the end. What I didn't know (since I rarely do any sort of detailed outline for things that I write), were many of the points, many of the characters, and many of the plot twists along the way.

For me, the thrill of writing is the discovery.

And I thought, what better way to discover than to start a story online and share it openly, not knowing where it might go.

So, in 2006 I wrote "The Online Journal of Peter O'Mallick" posted to a Blogger blog and started out telling his story via online blog entries in January of 2006.

Here's how the first journal entry opened:

Wednesday January 18, 2006. 10:23 PM

It's over. I can't believe it. Sarah won't speak to me. It's as if she blames me for her father's death sentence.

I can't say it's a new feeling, though. It's like all my life death has consumed the people close to me. First my parents, then my best friend, now Sarah's dad.

I've been where Sarah is now, but she won't let me help her – hell, she's not even talking to me.

Ever since her father announced to the family that he had an inoperable cancerous brain tumor so far advanced the doctors were giving him a 50/50 chance of living beyond one more month, she stopped talking to me, refused to see me and ignores my phone calls.

I've been four week now. Four, long, painful, horrible weeks. I think I'm going to die. I wish I was dead, actually, like so many of the people I've cared about.

Our school's guidance counselor suggested that I start this blog in order to try dealing with it.

So here I am, typing, trying to come to terms with it. But I don't want to write about how I feel – I keep stopping and just sit here smashing my fingers down on the keyboard, smashing my fists down on the desk. I want to break something, smash something, throw my computer monitor through the fucking window.

This is bullshit.

Sometimes Peter would post daily, sometimes multiple short posts in a day. Sometimes he would go missing-in-action for a couple of weeks.

But the story rolled out and began to gain followers who were interested in Peter's dilemma.

Comments on the blog (people pretended that Peter was real and reacted to him as if he were a real person), had an effect on Peter. He responded to them. He even wrote about the commenters. I enjoyed the strange interactive nature of this type of storytelling.

Along the way, because Peter's death curse is real, it seemed that almost everyone that he met fell victim to his tragic death curse. Colleagues and friends were dropping like flies all around Peter.

And then, because I was living in Hamilton, Ontario at the time, I thought it might be interesting to see if I could work with the local Literacy Council to raise money for them. I collaborated with them to host an auction where someone could get killed by Peter in my ongoing blog story.

The idea was that the winner of the auction would be written into the story, meet and interact with Peter, and then be killed by him; usually based on one of their real-life fears. I also would incorporate elements about them – their passion, their career, etc, into the tale. And they got to decide if I used their real name or a fictional one.

I ended up killing off two real people in the blog (and, the novel).

It was great fun.

Not just for me, but also for the people I killed, who got a special thrill out of that.

The online story went on for nine months.

Shortly after it finished, I pitched a novelization of Peter's story to a publisher who was interested in it. It was eventually published as the novel I, DEATH that was broken into three main parts. *Part One*: Peter's Journal. *Part Two*: POV of a major bad-guy reading Peter's journal. *Part Three*: Good Guy VS Bad Guy.

And, in the ramp-up to the release of the novel, I was regularly attending a conference in Niagara Falls, New York called *Eerie-Con*. It's a great little con (of usually less than 100 people) and I had the chance, over the years to meet and hang out with many great writers there, including Joe Haldeman, Larry Niven and Kevin J. Anderson. (Kevin and I bonded over craft beer and are still good friends to this day. In fact, just this morning, he texted me a couple of pictures of some beers he is enjoying in Wales while he's there as a guest of a science fiction convention).

Eerie-Con had a "People and Things" Auction that support this con and helped them afford having big name science-fiction, fantasy and horror authors as guest of honor.

I decided to auction off the chance to be a feature character killed by Peter in a stand-alone story that I would launch the following year at Eerie-Con as a "limited to 100 copies" chapbook.

Michael Bass won the auction. So, I met with him for coffee and gathered info about him. He was a part-time comedian, he was a huge hockey fan, he enjoyed brutally honest humor. He was also afraid of heights. I incorporated all of those elements into the story, and, came up with "Collateral Damage" a stand-alone story that takes place in a timeline between Chapters 6 and 7 of Part III of the novel *I, Death*.

I am planning a sequel to *I, Death* eventually. But I so enjoy the way that the character of Peter O'Mallick can allow me to kill real people who find a thrill in that. I can imagine that there'll be many more stand-alone Peter O'Mallick tales to write in the near future.

Perhaps he might become *your* friend one day.

Conclusion: Stranger Things Have Happened

Thanks for taking this little walk through the preceding pages with me and meeting some of the strangers and the strange encounters that had been documented.

If you enjoyed this collection, I would greatly appreciate if you left an honest review. It might seem like a small thing, but the one or two minutes it takes goes an incredibly long way towards helping a writer. Reviews and ratings really do help. So thanks, in advance.

And, if you're so inclined to send me a note to let me know what you thought, that would be wonderful too. It does mean a lot to me.

My email is mark@markleslie.ca. You can also, of course, sign up for my newsletter at www.markleslie.ca to stay informed of my new releases and get a full-sized eBook for free.

On the other hand, if you weren't satisfied with what you read, I'm happy to receive an email from you just the same. Your experience and thoughts are just as important. I'm constantly looking to grow as a writer, and learning why a story didn't work for a reader can be an important part of that process.

In either case, thanks for accompanying me on this stroll together as I introduced you to some strangers that I consider friends. Perhaps, one day, you and I shall encounter each other either between the digital pages of another book, or maybe in person at some bookish event somewhere out in the real world. If that happens, do say hello. After all, we've shared all these words together. You and I are no longer strangers.

Mark Leslie,
March 2021

About the Author

Mark Leslie is a writer, editor, and bookseller who was born and grew up in Sudbury, Ontario, spent many years in Ottawa, Ontario and currently lives in Southern Ontario. Claiming that he has always been frightened of the monster under his bed, Mark loves crafting eerie and creepy tales that follow the "what if" questions that occur to him every time he takes a peek into the shadows. And he spends a lot of times looking at the shadows and listening for the screams. You can learn more about Mark and sign up for his author newsletter at **www.markleslie.ca**.

Selected Other Books by Mark Leslie

Novels

A Canadian Werewolf in New York
Stowe Away
Fear and Longing in Los Angeles
Evasion
I, Death

Short Story Collections

One Hand Screaming
Active Reader
Nobody's Hero

Anthologies (as Editor)

Campus Chills
Tesseracts Sixteen: Parnassus Unbound
Fiction River: Editor's Choice
Fiction River: Feel the Fear
Fiction River: Feel the Love
Fiction River: Superstitious
Obsessions

Non-Fiction / Paranormal / Ghost Stories

Haunted Hamilton
Spooky Sudbury
Tomes of Terror
Creepy Capital
Haunted Hospitals
Macabre Montreal